W9-CCW-579

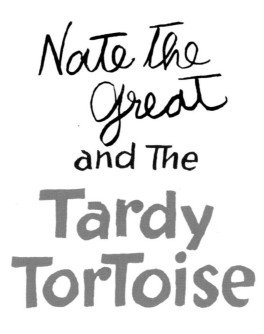

Nate the Great
and The
Tardy
TorToise

by Marjorie Weinman SharmaT
and Craig SharmaT

illusTraTed by Marc SimonT

Delacorte  Press

Published by
Delacorte Press
Bantam Doubleday Dell Publishing Group, Inc.
1540 Broadway
New York, New York 10036

Library of Congress Cataloging-in-Publication Data

Sharmat, Marjorie Weinman.
    Nate the Great and the tardy tortoise / by Marjorie Weinman Sharmat
and Craig Sharmat ; illustrations by Marc Simont.
        p.   cm.
    Summary: As more and more of his flowers display the bite marks of a
wandering tortoise, Nate sets out to uncover the mystery of the reptile's
origins.
    ISBN 0-385-32111-2
    [1. Turtles—Fiction.   2. Mystery and detective stories.]
I. Sharmat, Craig.   II. Simont, Marc, ill.   III. Title.
PZ7.S5299Navk   1995
[E]—dc20   94-49607
                                                                      CIP
                                                                       AC

The text of this book is set in eighteen-point Goudy Old Style.
Book design by Julie E. Baker

Manufactured in the United States of America
September 1995
10 9 8 7 6 5 4 3 2 1

For my parents,
who patiently took me
under their shell

—C. S.

I, Nate the Great, am a detective.
This morning I did not have
a case to solve.
I woke up late.
I stretched.
My dog Sludge stretched.

We looked out the window.
The sun was shining.
The birds were singing.
A tortoise was eating.
A tortoise was eating
the flowers in my garden.

I do not own a tortoise.
Sludge does not
own a tortoise.
Sludge and I rushed out
to the backyard.
The tortoise started to eat
a petunia.
A bite here.
A bite there.
He started to eat a daisy.
A bite here.
A bite there.
I, Nate the Great,
like to look at flowers.
Soon there would not be
any flowers to look at.

I stared at the tortoise.

He was green.

He had a thick shell.

And a big appetite.

He did not have any teeth.

But he did good work without them.

I knew I must take him away.

But what would I
do with him?

"You must live somewhere," I said.

"You must have an address
and a telephone number."

I knew that a tortoise can live
for a very long time.

This tortoise could be a hundred years old.

He should know where he lives by now.

He started to crawl away.

Slowly.
Very, very slowly.
Was he on his way home?
No. He was on his way
to eat my violets.
This tortoise was lost.
He needed help.

I said, "I, Nate the Great,
have never taken a case
for anyone who is green
and has a thick shell.
But I must find out
where you live
and take you there."
I got dressed.
I wrote a note to my mother.

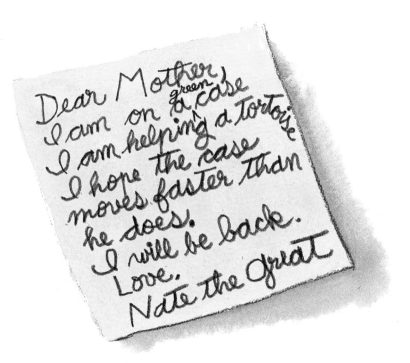

Dear Mother,
I am on a green case
I am helping a Tortoise
I hope the case
moves faster than
he does.
I will be back.
Love,
Nate the Great

I, Nate the Great, got a box.
I put lots of holes in it.
Then I put the tortoise in the box.
"I am taking you home,"
I said. "Wherever that is."
Where *was* his home?
I was thinking.
This tortoise is slow.
Perhaps he did not crawl
very far from home.

Perhaps he lives near here.
But he knows how to find food.
He could have been crawling
and eating for days.
He could have eaten his way
from the other side of town.
This tortoise could live anywhere!
I spoke to Sludge.
"This is a strange pet.
Who would own a strange pet?"
Sludge knew the answer.

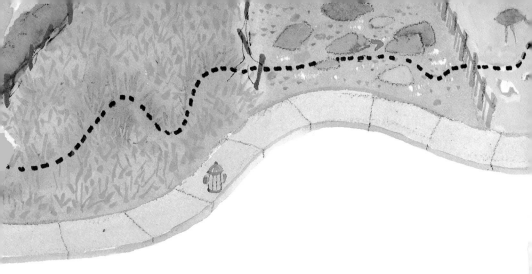

We rushed to Rosamond's house
with the box.
We walked
up the front steps.
Sludge sniffed
the steps.
Step by step.
I bent down to see
what Sludge was sniffing.
It was a trail of crumbs.
They led to the front door.
Sludge scratched on the door.

Rosamond opened it.
She was holding two crumbling
cupcakes.
Her cats, Little Hex, Plain Hex,

Big Hex, and Super Hex, were
eating crumbs from the floor.
"I have brought over
a lost pet," I said.
"Why, thank you," Rosamond said.
She opened the box
and saw the tortoise.
"This is not a cat,"
she said. "It is green
and has a shell.
I do not want it."
"This is not a gift," I said.
"I found this tortoise and
I am looking for his home.
Do you know anybody who
has lost a pet?"
"I heard that Claude lost
something," Rosamond said.

"But I don't know what it is.
Claude is always losing things."
"You are losing your cupcakes,"
I said. "They are turning
into crumbs."
"These are tuna fish cupcakes,"

Rosamond said. "Want some?"
I, Nate the Great, had not
eaten breakfast.
I was hungry.
But I was not *that* hungry.
Sludge was licking up the crumbs.
It was time to leave.
I said good-bye to Rosamond.
Sludge sniffed his way
down the steps.

Then we went to Claude's house.
Claude opened the door.
I stared at him.
There was something missing.
He was not wearing a sock
on his left foot.
"Have you lost a tortoise?" I asked.
"No," Claude said. "I have lost
my sock."
"Do you know anybody who owns
a tortoise?"
"I know that Pip and Oliver
and Esmeralda and Annie
do not own a tortoise,"
Claude said. "They do not
have my sock either.
Can you look for it?"

"I, Nate the Great,
am on a case.
I must find out
where a tortoise lives."
"My case is bigger," Claude said.
"My sock is size eleven
and a half."

"I cannot look for it,"
I said.
"I will give you a clue,"
Claude said. "The sock matches
the one on my right foot."
"Good idea," I said.
Sludge and I walked away.
Claude yelled after us.

"If you find my sock,
and it doesn't look
as good as my right sock,
I don't want it.
I need a match."
I, Nate the Great,
needed some pancakes.
Sludge needed a bone.
We went home.

I took the tortoise out
of the box.
He crawled around the kitchen.
Slowly.
Very, very slowly.
I made pancakes.
I gave Sludge a bone.
The tortoise looked at me.
Was that a hungry look?
"You are full of flowers,"
I said.
He kept looking.
I gave him a piece of pancake.
He took a little bite.
"Your owner must wonder
where you are and when
you are coming home,"
I said. "You are one

tardy tortoise."
I, Nate the Great,
ate a pancake and thought.
I needed a clue.
What did I know
about this tortoise?

Did he have any
friends or relatives?
How about hobbies?
I knew that he
liked flowers,
crawled very slowly,

and kept his secrets.
That was it.
This tortoise was never
going to get anywhere.
He was never going to be
President of the United States
or captain of the track team.
He was just a pet.
Like Sludge.
Hmmm.
Suddenly I knew what to do!
And where to look.
"This case is almost solved,"
I said to Sludge.
"I know who would know
where this tortoise lives."
I picked up the tortoise
and put him back in the box.

"Let's go," I said.
I, Nate the Great, and Sludge
rushed to the veterinarian
with the box.
"Tortoises must come here
just like most pets do," I said.
"There should be a record
of where this tortoise lives."
We walked into the waiting room.
It was full of dogs, cats,
and people.

The cats were meowing.
The dogs were barking.
One dog was barking the loudest.
It was Annie's dog, Fang.
He looked mad.
"Fang has a sore tooth,"
Annie said. "Look!"
I, Nate the Great,
did not want to look
at Fang's tooth.
"I am here on a case," I said.

I opened the box.
"I need to ask the vet
where this tortoise lives."
"Oh, a tortoise,"
Annie said. "I have
never seen one here."
"I have never seen one
here either," I said.

"But they do not meow.
They do not bark.
And they probably come
here in a box.
A tortoise could be here
and we would not see
or hear him."
"Yes," Annie said.
"But a tortoise is a reptile.
This place is not for reptiles,
birds, goldfish, goats, pigs,
wolves . . ."
"How do you know?" I asked.
"Because they thought Fang
was a wolf
the first time I brought him.
That's when I found out
who doesn't get in."

I, Nate the Great, sat down
next to a noisy cat.
This case was going
slower than the tortoise.
This case had come to
a dead end.
There was only one more thing
I could do.
I could get the name of
a reptile vet and go there.

And walk into a waiting room
filled with rattlesnakes,
boa constrictors, lizards,
alligators, crocodiles,
and other creepy creatures.
Some of them have
sharper fangs than Fang.
I had seen enough bites today.
I did not want to see any more.
Especially on me.

This case had begun with bites.

The tortoise was biting my flowers.

Biting . . .

Hmmm.

Perhaps that was a *clue*!

But what could I do with it?

I looked at Sludge.

He was the only dog in the room

who was not barking.

He was sniffing.
I thought about him sniffing
the trail of tuna fish
cupcake crumbs.
A *trail.*
Did *that* mean something?
All at once
I, Nate the Great, knew
that the tortoise
and Sludge
had given me the clues
I needed to solve this case.
We rushed home.
We went into the backyard.
I pulled out my magnifying glass.
"We are looking for a trail,"
I said. "A trail of bite marks.
On the flowers."

I looked to the right.
There were no bite marks.
I looked to the left.
I saw bite marks
shaped like little u's.
On flower after flower.

"Follow those u's!"
I said to Sludge.
"The tortoise ate his way
to our house. So we will
follow the trail
of bites backward
until we reach his house."
Sludge and I crept through
my garden.
Past the u's
on the petunias,
on the daisies.
On this flower and that flower.
Then the flowers stopped.
So did Sludge and I.
"The trail stops here,"
I said, "and the cement
walk starts. The tortoise

did not bite cement. We must
go to the yard next door."
Sludge and I rushed
to the next yard.
We saw flowers.
And we saw u's.
"This is easy," I said.
"This trail leads straight
to another yard."

Sludge and I made our way
to the next yard.
Then we stopped.
"This is *not* easy," I said.
"This yard has no flowers.
There are only weeds and grass.
Are they on the tortoise's menu?"
Sludge and I peered down.
We did not see any u's.
But we did see a trail.
Of dirt.
Where weeds had been.

Where grass had been.
The trail zigzagged.
Sludge and I zigzagged.
We zigzagged to
the other side of the yard.
The tortoise had munched
and crunched his way
from end to end.
Then the trail stopped.
More cement.
"On to the next yard," I said.
The next yard was full of rocks.
But I saw something bright
on the ground.
Was it part of a flower?
I bent down to look.
It was Claude's sock.
It was full of holes.

"I, Nate the Great,
have just solved a case
I did not want to solve.
And found a sock Claude
will never want to wear."
I picked up the sock
and put it in my pocket.

"Rocks and a sock," I said.

"This yard is no help.

The trail is cold.

But we will not give up.

On to the next yard!"

The next yard was full

of statues.

Snow White and the Seven Dwarfs.

Five flamingos.

And three ducks.

There was nothing alive

or green

or growing.

The tortoise could not

have eaten here.

"The trail is getting colder,"

I said. "Snow White,

the Seven Dwarfs, five flamingos,

and three ducks
cannot help us find
the tortoise's home.
But, I, Nate the Great,
will never give up."
Sludge wagged his tail.

We went to the next yard.
It was a mess.
I saw pieces of flowers.
Pieces of weeds.
Pieces of grass.
The yard had been
bitten to death!
Sludge and I looked
at each other.

"I, Nate the Great, say
that the tortoise
must have eaten
many meals in this yard.
This must be his
favorite restaurant."
And suddenly I knew why.
I saw a fence with a sign on it.
BEWARE OF THE TORTOISE.
I opened the box.
I spoke to the tortoise.
"Welcome home!" I said.
"The case is solved."
I took the tortoise
out of the box.

Suddenly a lady came
from behind the fence.
She ran toward us.
"Speedy, did you escape
under the fence again?
You are late for lunch."

Beware of
The Tortoise

"Lunch?" I thought.

"This tortoise never stopped
eating breakfast."

I handed Speedy to the lady.

Sludge's tail drooped.

He was sorry to see Speedy go.

So was I.

Speedy was a flower-wrecker,

a very slow mover,

and he had nothing to say.

But he was an okay tortoise.

"We will be back
to visit," I said.

"If you are here.

Remember where you live."

I reached into my pocket.

I pulled out Claude's sock.

I tied it to
the top of a stick.
I stuck the stick in the ground.
"A flag for you, Speedy.
This land is yours.
You ate it."
Then Sludge and I
and the empty box
started home.
Slowly.
Very, very slowly.